MY LiTTLE PONY The MOViE

PONY PIRATE PARTY!

Cover design by Elaine Lopez-Levine and Ching Chan.

Little, Brown and Company
Hachette Book Group
1290 Avenue of the Americas, New York, NY 10104
Visit us at lb-kids.com
mylittlepony.com

First Edition: August 2017

LB kids is an imprint of Little, Brown and Company.
The LB kids name and logo are trademarks of Hachette Book Group, Inc.

The publisher is not responsible for websites (or their content) that are not owned by the publisher.

Library of Congress Control Number 2017942702

ISBNs: 978-0-316-55703-0 (pbk.), 978-0-316-44475-0 (Scholastic edition), 978-0-316-55706-1 (ebook), 978-0-316-55704-7 (ebook), 978-0-316-55701-6 (ebook)

Printed in the United States of America

CW

10 9 8 7 6 5 4 3 2 1

Licensed By:

Pony Pirate Party!

Adapted by Magnolia Belle
Based on the Screenplay by Meghan McCarthy and Rita Hsiao
Produced by Brian Goldner and Stephen Davis
Directed by Jayson Thiessen

New York Boston

Princess Twilight Sparkle, Pinkie Pie, Fluttershy, Applejack, Rainbow Dash, Rarity, and Spike are helping prepare for the first ever Friendship Festival in Canterlot. Everypony is super excited!

Suddenly, a dark ship lands in Canterlot. Out steps Commander Tempest Shadow, who demands that the princesses give their magic to her.

Tempest works for the Storm King, an evil ruler who seeks to add this magic to his own. She uses orbs to turn the princesses to stone until the Storm King arrives.

Luckily, Princess Twilight Sparkle and her closest friends are able to escape! Now on the run from Tempest and her powerful Storm Guards, the ponies and Spike are on a quest beyond Equestria to find help for Canterlot.

After a long trip, Twilight spots an airship and shouts,
"Look! It's about to take off. Everypony, get on board!"

Thanks to her quick thinking, the friends all manage to stow away on the airship and escape the clutches of the Storm King's minions.

While the ponies and Spike are certainly happy to be away from Tempest—and even happier to be in the air, where it might be harder for her to catch up—they are in a new place. They look around, hopeful for some clues about their newest predicament.

Oh no! There is some rustling on the top deck. They rush to get into hiding places—just in case.

When the ponies finally spot some of the ship's crew, Applejack whispers, "What do ya think, Twilight? Should we come out of hiding and just ask 'em to take us with them?"

"I don't know," Twilight says. "They could be dangerous—"

Before she is able to finish her thought, they are discovered by one of the crew. He's a great big parrot named Boyle, and he alerts Captain Celaeno. The ponies are terrified!

"Eh, Cap'n? We supposed to be shipping livestock today?" Boyle asks, pointing at the ponies.

Captain Celaeno exclaims, "Looks like we have stowaways!"
Other parrots hear the commotion and come running to see.
There's Murdock, who has a fake beak; Lix Spittle, who has a
fake tail; Grin, who wears an eye patch; and Boyle.

"*Squawk.* Oh, it's ponies! *Squawk!*"

Captain Celaeno pulls out a book and begins leafing through it. "Let's see," she says. "Storm King's rule book says that in this scenario...throw 'em overboard!"

The ponies begin to panic. Pinkie Pie smiles and talks through her clenched teeth. "Uh, Twilight, what do we do now? Not all of us can *F-L-Y*."

"I'm thinking, Pinkie," Twilight Sparkle says.

Grin lowers the ship's gangplank. The ponies gasp as the parrots start to urge them toward the plank. Just as they are about to shove the ponies overboard, Boyle blows a loud whistle!

Captain Celaeno stops the parrots and says, "All right, that's lunch. Come on, everybody, you got fifteen minutes. Scarf it down."

"Oh boy, I'm hungry!" Boyle shouts.

The parrots all head toward the ship's galley to eat. The ponies are relieved, but definitely confused.

Rainbow Dash's stomach rumbles. She's so hungry! "Say, can we have some food, too?" she asks the captain. Captain Calaeno opens the rule book again.

"Well, what does it say, Cap'n?" Lix Spittle squawks.

The captain thumbs through the entire book, searching. "Food…food…food. *Hmm*. Well, nothing here says you can't!"

"Awesome!" Rainbow Dash shouts. The ponies all cheer.

Plop! **The parrots scoop gruel onto plates for the ponies, who are still pretty confused about why the parrots dropped everything to eat.**

Rainbow Dash asks, "So, you were about to toss us overboard, and you stopped for a lunch break?"

Boyle answers, "Storm King only allows one break a day for meals, so when the lunch whistle blows, you gotta take it. Then it's back to hauling goods."

Twilight Sparkle gets an idea. She pulls out her map of Equestria and waves it before Captain Celaeno. "Since you are a delivery ship, can you deliver *us* to safety?" she asks.

The captain refers to her rule book again. "Sorry. We do what the Storm King orders. Or we suffer his wrath."

Rainbow Dash frowns. "Wait a minute," she says. "You weren't always delivery birds, were you?"

Captain Celaeno replies, "Oh no. We used to be much more adventurous." Then she goes to a poster of the Storm King that's hanging on the wall and reveals a pirate flag underneath!

Rainbow Dash squeals, "Whoa! You used to be pirates?!"

Boyle says, "Uh, we prefer the term *swashbuckling treasure hunters*."

"So…pirates," Rainbow Dash says.

"You birds have to make a choice!" she announces. "You can let some lame Storm King tell you how to live your lives, or you can be *awesome* again!"

Boyle scratches his head and asks, "What do you mean 'be awesome again,' little blue pony?"

"I mean, be pirates again!"

The captain perks up. "You have no idea how hard it's been to stick to this dull routine that the Storm King forced on us."

Rainbow Dash kicks up her enthusiasm. She says, "Don't let him rob you of who you are! Be awesome! It's all up to you!"

Captain Celaeno orders, "Come on, pirates! Let's show these little ponies how it's done!"

The crew sings while they get to work. The airship's colorful sails unfurl, and the ponies are amazed. They even join in on the pirate work. Pinkie Pie shouts, "*Yarr*, we're real scallywags now, 'ey, Cap'n?!"

"Thank you, ponies!" Captain Celaeno says. "You will always have a friend in us pirates. Any time you need help, call on us and we'll be there on the spot—so long as you mark it with an X!"

The pirates are so grateful to Rainbow Dash and the other ponies that they alter their course.

The ponies all laugh and cheer. Rainbow Dash explodes with excitement over their new pirate friends. She soars around the ship and makes a Sonic Rainboom in the sky for all to see!

But Tempest sees it, too, and is still on their tails....

Princess Twilight Sparkle, Rainbow Dash, Rarity, Applejack, Fluttershy, Pinkie Pie, and Spike have a long journey ahead of them, but with the help of new friends like Captain Celaeno and her crew, they can do anything!